MASON GRACE'S magical laces

WILLOW EVANS
illustrated by
TOM KNIGHT

For my mum - T.K.

For Simon x - W.E.

HODDER CHILDREN'S BOOKS
First published in Great Britain in 2022
by Hodder and Stoughton

10 9 8 7 6 5 4 3 2 1

Illustrations by Tom Knight

A CIP catalogue record for this book is available
from the British Library.

ISBN 978 1 44495 700 6

Printed and bound in China

MIX
Paper from
responsible sources
FSC www.fsc.org   FSC® C104740

HODDER CHILDREN'S BOOKS
An imprint of Hachette Children's Group
Part of Hodder and Stoughton
Carmelite House, 50 Victoria Embankment,
London EC4Y 0DZ

An Hachette UK Company
www.hachette.co.uk
www.hachettechildrens.co.uk

MASON GRACE'S
magical Laces

WILLOW EVANS
illustrated by
TOM KNIGHT

Hodder Children's Books

Mason Grace had never won a race.
He had never scored a goal in football. He had never quite gotten the ball in the hoop. So he decided it was best not to try.

Mason liked to watch from the sidelines with Billy Bunny, his most favourite toy.

Mason's best friend Afia **always** won races. She was always picked first to be on a team. And she always tried to get Mason to join in.

But it was no use.

There were lots of games that Mason did like to play.
And sometimes he would even win!

SILLIEST
FACE
COMPETITION
~~RAINING~~
~~RAYNING~~
CURRENT CHAMPION
MASON

But sports were not for Mason.

When the Big Summer Sports Day was announced, Afia was very excited, but Mason was **NOT.**

"It's a chance to have fun and try out some new sports," said Mr Block. "Everyone will be taking part!"

This gave Mason a wobbly feeling in his tummy.

What if he trips and falls?

What if people laugh?

What if he loses at **everything?**

Back at home, Mason was still feeling worried about Sports Day.

"You just have to join in and try your best," said Gran. "It's all about having fun! There are so many sports you haven't even tried."

Mason shook his head. "I think I'll just watch."

Suddenly, Gran had an idea. "There might be something in my closet that will change your mind . . ."

Mason followed Gran. He had NEVER been in Gran's special closet.

Gran's closet was brimming from floor to ceiling with clothes and shoes for every occasion – and every type of sport!

"You know me – always trying something new," laughed Gran.
"You won't find any trophies in here, but I always give it my best shot."

Gran reached for a small box and passed it to Mason.

Opening the box, Mason saw lots of **bright, colourful, glowing** shoelaces!

"These magical laces will have you running those races in no time," said Gran.

"Will they help me to win the races?" asked Mason.

"Well, they will certainly help get your heart racing!" Gran winked. "But first, you need to learn how to tie them yourself."

Gran looped a second pair of laces round each of Billy Bunny's ears. Suddenly, he sprang to life!

Billy Bunny helped Gran to show Mason how to tie his laces.

"First make a big X
by crossing each lace.
Thread one end in through
the gap at the base.

Pull tightly, and this is
where Billy comes in. . .
Make loops just like bunny
ears, each long and thin.

Cross over the ears,
still holding them tight.
Thread one under the other –
you'll soon get this right!

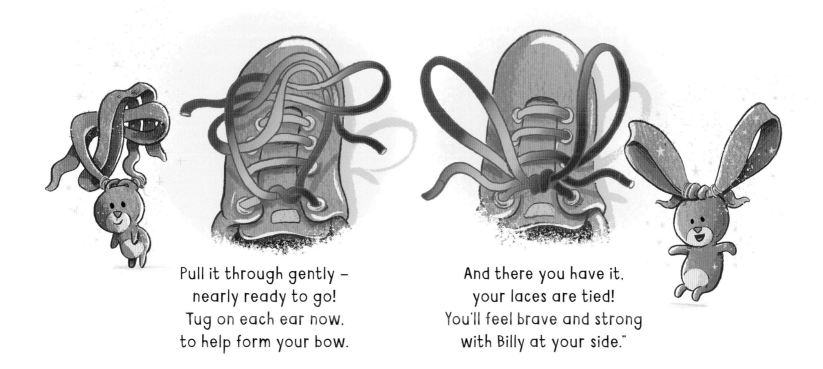

Pull it through gently –
nearly ready to go!
Tug on each ear now,
to help form your bow.

And there you have it,
your laces are tied!
You'll feel brave and strong
with Billy at your side."

Mason loved his new magical
laces. He and Billy Bunny
played outside all weekend.
Mason even got the
ball in the hoop after lots of tries!

But the night before the big Sports Day, Mason
got the wobbly feeling in his tummy again.

"Remember," said Gran, "tomorrow isn't about winning.
It's about joining in and trying your very best!"

Gran turned off the light, and with the soothing glow
of Billy Bunny's magical bows, Mason felt much better.

The next morning, the Big Summer Sports Day started bright and early. Mason proudly tied his laces, and lined up for the first race.

"If the bean bag falls off your head," said Mr Block, "you must go back to the start!

READY, SET ... GO!"

REFRESHMENTS

As the race began, Afia stormed ahead. Mason followed close behind when suddenly . . .

. . . the bean bag slipped off his head!

Mason looked down at his magical laces. "They must be broken," thought Mason. "They were supposed to help me win the races."

Just as he was about to give up, Mason heard his name being called from the sidelines.

"Just try your best, Mason!" Gran cheered as she waved Billy Bunny up in the air.

Mason picked up his bean bag and hurried back to the start, where lots of his friends were starting again too.

Giggling, everyone eventually made it past the finish line.

Mason didn't win, but he had fun and his heart was racing so fast he could hardly speak!

"See, those laces really did help you to get your heart racing!" called Gran as Mason dashed off to join in with the egg and spoon race.

After the races was the chance to try out some other sports.

Mason started to feel nervous again, but as he
retied his laces with Billy Bunny's help, he
knew he would give it his best.

Mason spent the afternoon . . .

bouncing

wiggling

dribbling

skipping

And soon, Mason didn't even need his magical laces to feel confident. He took off his shoes and headed right into . . .

jumping

shimmying

tumbling

balancing

On the way home, Mason and Afia admired the shiny new medals they were given for taking part in their first ever sports day.

"You're both winners in my eyes!" said Gran.

"It's not about winning, Gran!" laughed Mason.
"It's about joining in and having fun!"

Mason Grace still hadn't ever won a race. But
from then on, he knew he would always join in.
Because trying your best was easy with your
friends by your side and . . .

. . . there were lots more sports to try!